W9-BYJ-931

Easy words to read

Ted in a red bed

Phil Roxbee Cox

Illustrated by Stephen Cartwright

Edited by Jenny Tyler

Language consultant:

Marlynne Grant

BSc, CertEd, MEdPsych, PhD, AFBPs, CPsychol

There is a little yellow duck to find on every page.

SCHOLASTIC INC.

New York Toronto London Auckland Sydney
Mexico City New Delhi Hong Kong

No part of this publication may be reproduced in whole or in part, or stored in a retrieval system, or transmitted in any form or by any means, electronic, mechanical, photocopying, recording, or otherwise, without written permission of the publisher. For information regarding permission, write to Usborne Publishing Ltd., Usborne House, 83-85 Saffron Hill, London, EC1N 8RT, England. First published in Great Britain in 1999 by Usborne Publishing Ltd. • ISBN 0-439-23407-7 • Copyright © 1999 by Usborne Publishing Ltd. All rights reserved. Published by Scholastic Inc., 555 Broadway, New York, NY 10012, by arrangement with Usborne Publishing Ltd. The name Usborne and the device ⊕ are trademarks of Usborne Publishing Ltd.

SCHOLASTIC and associated logos are trademarks and/or registered trademarks of Scholastic Inc.

12 11 10 9 8 7 6 5 4 3   1 2 3 4 5 6/0 • Printed in the U.S.A.   08 • First Scholastic printing, March 2001

Ted likes to shop.

Ted stops. Ted hops.
Ted smiles a big smile.

3

"I like this bed," thinks Ted.

"I like red wood. Red wood is good."

"I want to see more."

"Try the red bed," says Fred.

"Oh, yes," says Ted.

Ted slips
his feet
under
the sheet.

He flops on the pillow.

The pillow is yellow.

"I need this bed, Fred!" grins Ted.

"It is a nice price," smiles Fred.

Now it's Ted's bed, not Fred's bed.

Ted feels sleepy.
Ted falls asleep.

Ted has a dream.

He bobs down a stream.

Fred's
Beds

Ted has a dream.

He bobs on a wave.   into a cave.

Ted has a dream.

He can
fly in the sky!

Ted has a dream.

He is back by the stream.

Ted wakes up with a snore.

He's not in the store any more.

Ted is home. His bed is home too.

"This red bed must be a magic red bed!"